Stanley Bagshaw
and the short-sighted football trainer

By
Bob Wilson

Barn Owl Books

D1087827

In Huddersgate (famed for its tramlines),
Up north where it's boring and slow,

Stanley Bagshaw resides with his Grandma
At number 4 Prince Albert Row.

RY MORNING

AND AFTER TEA

Thanks Grandma

They're playing football in the Milk Cup.

What a terrible waste of milk!

Our Stanley was quite keen on football
And for weeks he had been saving up
To see his team, Huddersgate Albion
Play against 'Spurs' in the cup.

These pigs have an odd way of eating!

They were selling the tickets on Tuesday.
Stan was up by a quarter to eight.
He thought he might be the first in the queue.
But......

Eee-aye-addio....
We're playing in the cup.

He's a child of Simple pleasures

In fact he had quite a long wait.

When at last Stanley got to the window,
And he took out his money to pay.
The man said....

Sorry son,
I've just sold the last one.

And our Stan didn't know what to say.

I've decided to save up for a bike instead.

Not hungry, Stan?

I'm feeling tired. I think I'll have an early night.

On the day of the match it was sunny
Stan watched all the crowds bustle by

With their flags and their scarves and their ratt[les]
And he said to himself

I won't cry.